SCARLETT &CRIMSON

The Secret Ingredient

by Allyson Black
illustrated by Shane L. Johnson

Simon Spotlight
New York London Toronto Sydney

Based on the concept "Scarlett & Crimson" by Ged Backland

This book was written in collaboration with Bobbi JG Weiss, David Cody Weiss, and Orli Zuravicky.

SIMON SPOTLIGHT
An imprint of Simon & Schuster Children's Publishing Division
1230 Avenue of the Americas, New York, New York 10020
© 2010 Coolabi & Ged Backland. All rights reserved, including the right of reproduction in whole or in part in any form. SIMON SPOTLIGHT and colophon are registered trademarks of Simon & Schuster, Inc.
For information about special discounts for bulk purchases, please contact Simon & Schuster Special Sales at 1-866-506-1949 or business@simonandschuster.com.
Manufactured in the United States of America. 1009 WOR
First Edition 10 9 8 7 6 5 4 3 2 1
ISBN 978-1-4169-6058-4
Library of Congress Control Number 2009928376

MONDAY
Lunchtime

"Can any of you clue me in on what Generation Fix is?" Pepper White asked the table full of Darqlings as he set down his lunch tray. "I caught some buzz about it in the hallway, on the way here."

That particular table in the cafeteria was the home base for kids at V. Price Memorial Middle School who were into the Darq. The Darq philosophy was Scarlett Ravencraft and Crimson Hawthorne's way of making sense out of the often confusing world around them.

Darq had its signature style and music, as many school scenes did. But Darq was more than just that.

Scarlett and Crimson had built and uploaded their own DarqSpace website. The home page declared a simple mission statement:

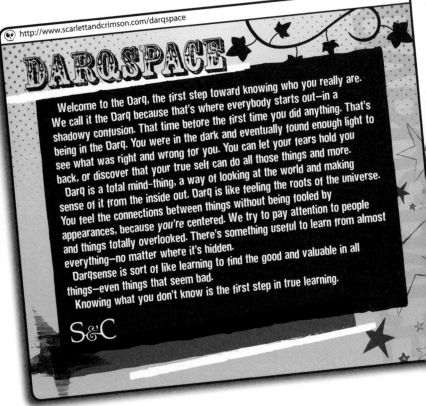

http://www.scarlettandcrimson.com/darqspace

DARQSPACE

Welcome to the Darq, the first step toward knowing who you really are. We call it the Darq because that's where everybody starts out—in a shadowy confusion. That time before the first time you did anything. That's being in the Darq. You were in the dark and eventually found enough light to see what was right and wrong for you. You can let your fears hold you back, or discover that your true self can do all those things and more.

Darq is a total mind-thing, a way of looking at the world and making sense of it from the inside out. Darq is like feeling the roots of the universe. You feel the connections between things without being fooled by appearances, because *you're* centered. We try to pay attention to people and things totally overlooked. There's something useful to learn from almost everything—no matter where it's hidden.

Darqsense is sort of like learning to find the good and valuable in all things—even things that seem bad.

Knowing what you don't know is the first step in true learning.

S&C

From there DarqSpace had rapidly expanded to feature gallery after gallery of fashion styles, a thriving forum posting the hottest news and rumors, advice columns, and music. Oh, yes, there was lots of music. And of course, Darq chat rooms galore.

Darq music found its spotlight in the middle school scene when Scarlett and Crimson's song, "A Light in the Darq," was chosen as the runner-up in the town's Battle of the Bands competition on Halloween. Composed and written by Crimson, "A Light in the Darq" became the genesis and heart of their band, DarqStarz. Scarlett played lead guitar and Crimson sat in on drums, with friends Pepper and Mac Bryant on keyboards and bass. Winslow Leek played tech wizard behind the curtain, capturing their unique sound and turning "A Light in the Darq" into the professional-sounding track that got it chosen as a top ten finalist.

"Hello? Anyone? What is Gen Fix?" Pepper repeated to the table.

"Gen Fix is this sweet new website that translates British babble-speak into plain American," Scarlett teased her English pal.

"Oh, translating to American is simple," Pepper replied, flashing his crooked half-smile. "Just replace every fifth word with 'like' or 'totally' and then sprinkle 'ummms' into otherwise grammatically perfect sentences. I'm, um, like, picking it up rather quickly myself, don't you think?"

Scarlett smirked. "Em, quite well indeed," she answered, mimicking Pepper's British accent.

Further down the table Emzie Zamora passed a folded note to her friend Tara Cartwright. Winslow stole a glance at Emzie, who gave him a broad wink in return. Their recently bloomed crush was still in the early awkward stage. He blushed and developed a sudden fascination with the Tater Tots on his plate.

Pepper flicked his eyes toward the rest of the table. "All joking aside, can you please help a fellow Darqling in distress?"

Scarlett meticulously patted the one red streak in her head of ebony hair into place. "Well, strange visitor from the land of, like, fish and chips, you probably grew up with thousands of totally moldy ancient traditions, right?" she said. "So, Community Service Week goes back to prehistoric times in Old Mill. I mean, like, my *mom* did it as a kid."

She turned to Crimson for backup. Normally, her BFF would already be tossing out her own quips. This morning, though, Crimson was clacking her fingernails on the table and staring into space with a slight frown.

"Cee?" Scarlett asked.

Crimson snapped her head around, her fuscia bows swinging wildly. "What? I'm fine," she said a little gruffly. "Of course I am. Why wouldn't I be?"

"Umm . . . Community Service Week?" Scarlett prompted. "Pepper's question?"

"Right. Ah, yeah. It's an annual thing where everybody tries to get everybody else involved with helping out in the community. For a week."

"Not surprising that they call it Community Service Week, then," Scarlett picked up with a dramatic roll of her eyes.

Crimson had her rhythm back now. "It's organized so that the kids from all the middle schools and high schools in the town sign up to help out with volunteer projects—"

"Like park cleanups, or making dinners that Wheelie Meals can deliver to shelters, like Cee and I are already going to do—"

"And there are tons of other really cool jobs," Crimson interrupted.

"Not only do you feel all warm and tingly inside from doing good deeds, but the school also awards Community Service Stars—"

"And extra civics credits that get added to your GPA, sort of like Advanced Placement–style bonuses," continued Crimson. "The more projects you participate in, the more credits you get. Oh, and the teachers totally give way less homework and no tests this week because they know we'll all be spending loads of time doing our community service."

Scarlett was ready to step in for the big finish. "And to top it all off, the town ropes off almost all of downtown and celebrates the end of Service Week with a huge Harvest Fair, total all-day block party. Students and town businesses set up booths and sell all this amazing stuff and delicious food. We're talking, like, miles of booths, and all the money raised gets donated to town projects that can totally use the cash."

"This year's biggie is the Old Mill Library computer lab upgrade," Crimson finished.

Pepper flashed his half grin. "A very educational and thorough explanation. Except that you left out what Gen Fix actually *is*."

"Oh, that's us," replied Scarlett. "Generation Fix, that is. We've got our own brand name already."

"I like it," said Pepper. He readjusted his shades and struck as noble a pose as he could in a plastic chair.

"There's going to be an assembly after lunch where we get to choose what projects we want to work on for the rest of the week," Emzie added.

"Why bother?" a snarky female voice broke in.

"Whatever you *dorklings* do is guaranteed to be a spectacle of pure fail." All eyes turned to see a crowd of Leetz strolling past the table. As usual, the "popular" girls and their jock escorts were dressed in the latest hot mall styles. All flash and no soul, but oh-so-fashionable.

"Don't discourage them, Paige," said Brianna, the Leetz's self-appointed Queen of the Scene. "If we're stuck having to do this boring Service Week stuff, at least we'll get some LOLs seeing our booth swarming with cool people while theirs looks like it's been hit by the Angel of Death."

"There *is* that," admitted Paige with a superior smirk.

Brianna smiled sweetly at the Darqlings. "Yes, it'll be pure fun watching them thrash their tiny fists in the air and cry their little emo eyes out."

"And your plan is totally foolproof." Casey laughed. "I mean, there's no way anyone can top your secret Kissing Booth!"

Brianna stared icy daggers at Casey, whose nickname, Casey the Clown, was well earned. Paige was less restrained. She whacked Casey with her plush pink bunny purse. "That was supposed to be a secret!" she hissed at him. "That's what the 'secret' part of 'secret plan' is all about!"

Casey bolted for the safety of Leetz Corner. The rest of the Leetz recomposed their attitudes and stalked after him.

"How can they possibly think *we're* emo!" Tara announced in shock. "They are so totally and completely clueless."

"That's exactly what makes them the Leetz, T," Crimson comforted.

"Dudes, I'll team up with you guys if you want," drawled Mac, who was trailing behind the Leetz on his way to the Darqling table.

"Totally, my good dude," Pepper said, giving Mac a lazy salute. "Check you out at the assembly, then."

"Cool," Mac said, dropping his lunch tray down with a bang.

At the far end of the table, two other Darqlings, Kaitlyn Daniels and Garrett Moretti, were whispering as they passed Emzie's note between them. Garrett spun it across the table toward Pepper, but it skidded past him and landed in Crimson's lap. The whisperers fell ominously silent.

Crimson unfolded the note and read:

Crimson's lips thinned and annoyance clouded her face, totally opposite from her normally cheery expression. "A surprise birthday party?" she growled. "For *me*? Did anybody think to even ask if I *wanted* a party? Scarlett, why did you tell everybody?" She stood up suddenly and scooped up her book bag. "Well, change of plans. I'm not *having* a birthday this year!"

Crimson ran off just as the class bell rang, leaving a table full of stunned faces. But Scarlett wasn't about to just sit there. Something strange was going on, and she was determined to get to the bottom of it. It was time for an intervention.

"Cee, wait just one minute," Scarlett shouted after her friend, catching up to her and locking her arm around Crimson's. "You don't get to do some big, diva-style storm-off with me. It's time for a little conference in the girls' room."

The twosome glided through the hallway in silence, turning left at the stairwell toward the girls' bathroom all the way at the end of the hall. It was usually less populated than the other one in that building, and the girls needed some serious privacy. Once they saw they had the place to themselves, Scarlett took her usual spot, perched on the windowsill, while Crimson pretended to fix her hair in the mirror.

"So," Crimson began, redoing one of her braids. "Now that you have me here, what's so important?"

"Cee, what's this about not celebrating your birthday?"

"Look, it's no biggie. I just don't feel like celebrating this year, that's all."

"What do you mean, 'it's no biggie'? You, like, *love* your birthday! It's only your most favorite day ever. I mean, I usually have to reserve you a year in advance because you're always so booked up on the big day celebrating with your mo—"

"Well that's not going to happen this year either."

"Oh, gosh, I'm sorry. I didn't mean to . . . do you want to talk about it?"

"Talk about what? There's nothing to say."

"Not even to me?"

"No, Ess, not even to you. Anyway, it doesn't matter what used to happen. Things change. This is now, and now I'm telling you I'm not having a birthday. So please just drop it!"

And with that Crimson stormed out of the bathroom, leaving a flushed and flabbergasted Scarlett behind.

Before they were Scarlett and the crew got to the gym,

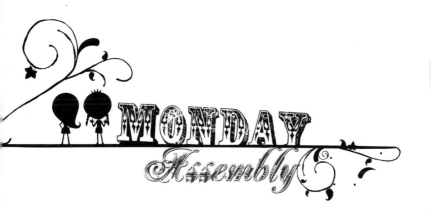

MONDAY Assembly

By the time Scarlett and the crew got to the gym, Crimson had already vanished into the crowd of kids pouring through the double doors.

Long tables lined the walls of the room, and more tables made a square in the center. Bold signs hung from each table, naming the different activities available, and helpful people stood by to answer questions. There were dozens of activities to choose from: neighborhood litter patrols, park cleanup squads, soup kitchen helpers, retirement home volunteers, and tons more.

"Anything grab you yet?" Winslow asked Pepper.

"Yeah, pretty much everything, mate," Pepper answered with his trademark crooked half grin. "I'm the foreigner, remember?" He spread his arms to take in all the bustle as students interacted with community organizers. "I feel like I'm on safari in deepest, darkest Yank suburbia." He pointed toward a table with a yellow plastic fire hydrant painted with bright purple polka dots. "I doubt that color scheme would go over well back home."

Scarlett burst out laughing at the sight of the hydrant. "Definitely needs some spiderwebs instead," she said. "Or bats."

"Bats are *always* in good taste," Crimson's voice said from behind them. Everyone spun around to look at her. Crimson continued as if nothing out of the ordinary had happened earlier. "I just signed up for that one. Mac, Pepper—feel like going all batty on the neighborhood with me?"

Scarlett was stunned for the second time that day. What happened to their original plan to make Wheelie Meals dinners together? Was Crimson—her best friend in the world—really *ditching* her to paint fire hydrants with someone else? Mac, Pepper, Emzie, and the others stood in an uncomfortable silence, hoping someone would break it soon.

"Cee, what happened to Wheelie Meals at Judy's Cookin' Nook?" Scarlett asked, trying to stay calm.

"What's a Cookin' Nook?" Pepper interjected, hoping his question would distract Scarlett from the flames that were burning holes through her cheeks.

"It's this, like, amazing little hole-in-the-wall café up on Golden Hill that all these creative people love to hang out at," Crimson answered with that same brittle brightness. "The owner, Judy—she calls herself Judy the Beauty on Duty—is an old friend of my m—er, family. Everything you'd ever want to know about Old Mill is served up hot and juicy at the Cookin' Nook."

"Yeah, and that's where Cee and I have been spending Service Week since forever," Scarlett finished. "So you're really not going to do it with me this year?"

Crimson smiled a pasted-on smile. "Sure, Ess. We can totally still do that too, if you want. I just thought it would be fun to do something different and get to know some fellow Darqlings a bit better while I'm at it."

Now Scarlett was even more confused than before. Though her best friend was still game to do Wheelie

Meals at Judy's, Scarlett was starting to feel like Crimson really had been trying to get out of it earlier. Was she really that mad over the whole birthday thing? Scarlett wasn't quite sure what to do. After all, nothing like this had ever happened between the two girls before.

"Well, Judy is really looking forward to having our help," Scarlett offered, trying to lighten things up. "So if you're still in, I'm still in."

"Sure, Ess. I'll meet you there later on." Then Crimson made a show of looking up at the wall clock. "Ah," she said. "Gotta run. See you guys at the maintenance shop this afternoon if you want to paint fire hydrants," she directed at Mac and Pepper. Then she headed toward the door, wiggling good-bye with her fingers.

"Anybody care to guess what just happened?" asked Emzie, her mouth and eyes forming shocked circles. Red spots flamed on Scarlett's cheeks as she stared at the floor. Nobody else spoke.

Winslow strolled up, staring at a clipboard in his hand. "Hey, gang," he said. "I found this cool recycling gig for us to do, and it's right across the street." He caught the sense of awkwardness in the air and blinked owlishly. "Uh . . . did I miss something?"

"Hard to say," said Pepper, staring at Crimson's retreating back. "I get the feeling that we all just did."

MONDAY
After School

As puzzled as Scarlett was by her friend's odd behavior, she tried not to let it dent her normally cheerful attitude. Whatever was bugging Crimson would come out when Crimson was good and ready to talk about it. At least she hoped it would. In the meantime, she was running late to meet Emzie and Winslow at Frankie's Recycling Depot.

Scarlett had never noticed that there was a recycling yard so close to V. Price Memorial Middle School. Of course, those big green curved recycle arrows painted on that yellow fence were kind of a big clue, she thought,

giggling to herself. She walked through the wide double gates into a dirt yard crammed with neatly stacked piles of, well, *everything*—old computers, monitors, newspapers, bags of yard clippings, bins of glass and plastic bottles, bald tires, you name it.

No sooner had Scarlett set foot in the yard than a pack of frantically barking dogs came racing around a corner. There were at least a dozen of them, led by a dark brown Saint Bernard–Labrador mix. Dachshunds and basset hounds scrambled between the legs of a German shepherd. A Chihuahua hopped like a

giant flea past a half-blind husky, who slowly sniffed a path forward. Other dogs showed signs of hard lives—scars, bent ears, arthritic joints. One beautiful auburn Irish setter hopped nimbly on three legs. Clearly somebody's heart was a mile wide.

A short, sharp whistle from deeper in the yard brought the pack to a sudden halt. Obedient but still yearning to greet the newcomer, the dogs whined as their attention flicked from Scarlett to the tall woman in overalls walking out of the shack that stood at the center of the yard.

"Bear-Bear!" the woman barked. "Where are your manners? How do we greet visitors?"

The lumbering old Bernard-Lab did an about-face and directed a hoarse bellow-bark at the rest of the pack. Immediately the rest of the dogs sat at attention, a half-dozen tails wagging on the ground and raising clouds of dust. "Don't be afraid of them," the woman said to Scarlett. "The worst they'd do is drown you in puppy slobber."

Scarlett leaned over to rake her fingers through Bear-Bear's dense ruff. "If that's my fate, then that's my fate. I loooove doggies," she crooned. "My best friend has an adorable Scottish terrier named Baskerville. He's the crankiest puppy on the planet; he actually *refuses* to give kisses!" She laughed as Bear-Bear jumped up, trying to lick her face. "You're just a big floppy baby, aren't you? Yes, you are, I can tell. Come give Scarlett some doggie-kisses." Bear-Bear lurched forward and flung his giant paws onto Scarlett's shoulders, his pink tongue swiping her cheek from chin to ear.

The rest of the pack took that as a green light to join in the fun. Scarlett let them swarm around her, nuzzling her hands, knees, and everything else they could reach. Inevitably, the mass of happy dogs toppled her backward. Giggling madly, she shrieked in mock panic, "Dogpile on Scarlett! Dogpile! Dogpile!"

"That's enough, beasties," the woman said firmly. "Take charge, Bear-Bear."

The big dog muscled the others away from Scarlett and cleared a space around her by barking doggie commands. With one last rusty bellow, he led the pack racing deeper into the maze of bins and black plastic bags, almost bowling over Winslow and Emzie as they came out of the shack. Emzie gave the dogs hearty thumping pats as they scrambled by. "Aren't they just the sweetest things?" she said. Winslow tried to look at ease around the dogs, but he clearly didn't know how to relate to their friendly rough-and-tumble.

"Frankie," the woman said, extending a hand to Scarlett. "Nice to meet ya. Welcome to the Recycling Depot."

Close up, Scarlett could see that Frankie was tanned and well muscled from her work outdoors. Her cropped hair swept up into a spiky purple fauxhawk.

"Scarlett Ravencraft," said Scarlett, shaking Frankie's hand. "I take it you've already met Emzie and

Winslow. We're here to help out for the week."

"And earn extra credits," Winslow added.

"Earning them is just what you'll be doing. Sorting glass bottles and aluminum cans isn't rocket science," said Frankie with a grin, "but there are tons of them to sort. Every bottle and can recycled is one piece of glass or metal that doesn't have to be made. And you may not believe it, but even those worn-out tires stacked over there can have a new life after they're ground up and mixed with asphalt—they become whole new roads." Her cell phone rang, its ringtone a classic Broadway show tune. "I've got to take this. Emzie and Winslow will show you what goes where, Scarlett. Have fun." She tapped her remote earpiece and began answering the caller's questions as she walked back to the shack.

Emzie and Winslow led Scarlett to the yard's drop-off gate and the bags of unsorted stuff that waited there. "Like Frankie said, cans go with cans, bottles go with bottles—divided by glass color, natch," Emzie said. "Repeat until there's nothing left to sort."

"Which is likely never," said Winslow, a bit daunted by the sheer volume of the recyclables in the yard. He headed for the electronic gadget stack.

Emzie shook her head. "The hard part is going to be stopping our mad scientist pal from adopting every last scrap."

Winslow called from across the yard, "Who'd want to dump all this? Most of it's perfectly good—just old."

"I rest my case," Emzie muttered to Scarlett. Louder, she told Winslow, "That's why we're *recycling* them."

"But, I mean, look at this," Winslow continued, inching closer to the girls with what appeared to be a bashed-up zip drive. "This is super salvageable. What would make someone throw this away?"

"I think maybe most people aren't as good as you are at, you know, putting computers together and stuff," Scarlett answered, laughing as she sorted through a pile of cans. "I mean, *that* looks pretty broken to me!" she continued, turning back around to face her friends.

After a few seconds, Scarlett noticed that they seemed less interested in her thoughts on the bashed zip drive and more in communicating with each other through a newfound language of winks. They wound up looking way more awkward than subtle, which she was pretty sure defeated the purpose.

"What's going on with you two?" Scarlett asked, smiling at her friends.

"Oh, uh, Emzie has something she wants to ask you," Winslow announced, shoving Emzie into the spotlight.

"Okay," Scarlett responded hesitantly. "What do you need? If you're having, ahem, relationship problems," she whispered into Emzie's ear, "I'm not sure I can help you. . . ."

"Ha, ha!" Emzie laughed awkwardly. "No, it's not *that*. It's just, well, um, Winslow and I were sort of wondering what happened today, you know, with Crimson? I mean, first she stormed out of the cafeteria all angry that you told us it was her birthday on Saturday, and then she was all weird with you at assembly. And now here we are, the *three* of us, no Crimson. It's just, um, kinda weird. So is everything okay?"

"Oh, *that*?" Scarlett began, turning back to face the pile of cans. "Everything's totally fine!" she announced, tossing a can into the recycling bin a little too emphatically. "Crimson's just, well . . . she's . . . it's like . . . she's just going through a thing, you know?"

"Oh, yeah, totally," Emzie replied, trying to comfort

her friend. "Winslow," she hinted, "don't you know *exactly* what Scarlett means?"

"Uh . . . I . . . um . . . sure. I mean, what?" he finally spat out, utterly confused.

"Look, guys," Scarlett said. "I really appreciate you asking, and it's totally sweet that you're worried, but Crimson and I are fine. Promise. She's just going through a thing and *I'm* going through a thing, and so our things are, like, overlapping in kind of an off way, but it'll all be fine. I swear."

"That makes total sense, Scarlett," said Emzie genuinely. "Well, just so you know, we're here for you if you ever want to, you know, talk."

"Thanks, guys. That means a lot, really. But for now, let's get to sorting some garbage. Otherwise we'll be here forever!"

While Emzie and Winslow shifted gears and began sorting paper goods, Scarlett stuck over by the cans, thinking about what had just transpired. With every can that she threw in the bin, she became more and more flustered. Were things with her and Crimson so off that even two computer junkies who spent their nights flirting with each others' computer-animated avatars had noticed it?

Just then Bear-Bear came snuggling up beside Scarlett, pushing his snout up toward her chin. "I guess you could tell that I was in need of some TLC, huh, li'l guy?" Scarlett whispered to her new friend. "Thanks, buddy, you're the best."

Across the street, inside the school's maintenance workshop, another crew of Darqlings was getting ready to start a new volunteer project.

"It's about time you showed," Crimson greeted Pepper and Mac with good humor as they walked into the workshop. "Didja get lost walking all the way around the school?"

"My lady's rapier wit hath woundeth me to the

quick," Pepper cried in his best Fakespearean accent as he clapped a hand over the pocket of his overshirt. "I bleed, I bleed."

"You *leak*, is more like it, dude," said Mac, pointing at the broken pen staining the pocket. Pepper gave a *yeep* and quickly removed the shirt.

"If we're done with the comedy part of the show, boys, it's time to get going. Mr. Kramer set me up with paints and stencils as well as a map of the neighborhood's fire hydrant locations before he had to run off and clean up a mess in the cafeteria," Crimson said.

Mac unrolled one of the stencils and stared at it in disbelief. "Are these dudes serious?" he said. "Polka dots?"

Pepper grabbed a corner of the paper to look closer. "I thought that sample in the auditorium was a joke, honest. Must we stand in public, painting such lame stuff?"

Crimson thumbed through the rest of the stencils. "Stripes . . . more dots . . . a lightning bolt . . . and, oh my—" She took the polka dot plan from Pepper and rolled it and the rest of the stencils into a tube, which she tossed on top of a worktable. "Get me a wheelbarrow, would you please, Mac?"

When Mac returned with the wheelbarrow, Crimson started loading it with cans of reflective paint and a deep tray of rollers and brushes. "Grab that fire hydrant map, boys, and let's see if our imaginations can come up with some better designs."

The nearest fire hydrant was at the gate of the teachers' parking lot near the side street. It was clear from even the quickest look that the grimy paint job had deep chips in it that revealed a history of different coats in reds or neon yellows. Crimson used a screwdriver to pry open a couple of paint cans. "Let's start out with something simple—a base coat of safety yellow with the hose attachments in robin's egg blue and those chains linking them picked out in fire engine red."

Pepper stared at the big hex bolts centering the screw-on hose fixtures. His crooked half grin crinkled his face. "I don't know, Hawthorne. My gut is telling me to turn those bolts into giant eyes."

Crimson fished out a can of pale blue paint and handed it to Pepper. "You can't deny your gut, my friend. Knock yourself out."

Soon the three of them were reaching around each

other, trying to paint the whole hydrant at once without messing up someone else's work or dribbling paint on themselves. Silly laughter soon followed. As Pepper dabbed black paint onto the big bolts to turn them into eyes, he wondered aloud, "Anyone happen to see what project, if any, the Leetz signed up for?"

Mac answered around a small paintbrush clenched between his teeth. "Last I saw, they were all signing up for the bleachers and sports field cleanup."

"Can't be," objected Crimson. "That sounds far too much like honest work for their delicate souls."

"Yah," agreed Pepper. "Not something a TV crew or fashion reporters would show up at."

Soon the first hydrant was done, bright paint gleaming wetly in the sunny fall afternoon. They put down their gear and stepped back to examine their creation. Crimson had painted the domed top of the hydrant to look like a red wool knitted cap. Below that, the hose-hookups-turned-into-eyes stared back at them.

Crimson stared at it critically. "It's okay enough, for a first try," she said.

Mac stood back to take it in. "There's something missing."

"No, not missing," Pepper said. "It's more like it's—it's—"

"Totally meh," Crimson finished. "Nothing really creative, much less meaningful or Darq, even."

"Well," Pepper drawled, "we *do* have a dozen more to practice on."

Crimson perked right up. "Right," she declared. "Let's do the next one as a totally retro spaceship."

The boys began piling brushes and cans into the wheelbarrow. "Look out, neighborhood," Crimson announced. "The Darqlings are out to deliver a total style smackdown on dullness everywhere!"

The farm reds sun was about to set, as Scarlett and Crimson approached.

MONDAY Evening

The fat red sun was about to set as Scarlett and Crimson approached Judy's Cookin' Nook from opposite corners of the street. A bright rainbow-striped awning shaded four outdoor tables, each with its own cheerful flower centerpiece. A small antique table to the left of the door offered lemon and cucumber infused water to make waiting more comfortable during breakfast and lunch rushes. The cafe didn't serve dinner, but it stayed open till seven. When Scarlett and Crimson arrived that evening, the late lunchers were still gossiping and watching the sunset.

The two friends stopped on either side of the door,

awkwardly facing each other, unsure of who should enter first. Scarlett was about to say something when suddenly the restaurant owner herself threw open the screen door and flung her arms around them both in a double hug. "Welcome, ladies, welcome. Absolutely delighted to see you! Come in, come in. Your table awaits."

The rich smell of homemade cooking surrounded the girls like incense as Judy hustled them into the main dining room. An old-fashioned lunch counter filled one side of the room, with antique chairs of mixed styles fastened atop the original aluminum stool bases. Dining booths ran along the outer walls, the upholstery redone patchwork-quilt-style. Some booths sported leather patches, others mainly denim. Beautiful paintings in vintage frames decorated the walls, all done by local artists and most of them inscribed to Judy. Every other square inch of space was covered with photos spanning twenty years. In an instant Scarlett and Crimson were settled in the first booth, Crimson being scooched in a little farther so Judy could sit as well.

Dressed in a retro fifties waitress uniform, Judy peered at them through rose-tinted owl glasses perched on a rather beaky nose. But when she smiled, which was nearly always, she radiated joyous energy into the room like a lighthouse beacon. She flipped out her order pad. "What can I get you darlings?"

"Nothing, really," Crimson said. "We're here to make dinners for Wheelie Meals, remember?"

"Oh yeah, that's right. But first, a cup of my famous hot chocolate," Judy replied, stepping behind the counter to fix the girls her specialty. "Actually, let's make 'em doubles. Something tells me you two are going to need the energy."

"But we didn't ask for—," Crimson began.

Judy shook her long, bony pointer finger back and forth in the air as punishment. "My kitchen, my rules," she said firmly.

Crimson replied with a reluctant "hmph" as Judy brought out their hot chocolates.

She grinned at Scarlett. "Her mother used to sit in that booth and make that same exact noise at me. Didn't soften me up then, either."

Crimson pouted. "No fair bringing Mom into this."

"Why not?" Judy shot back. "She was my best friend long before she became your mother. We roamed the plains when dinosaurs ruled the earth."

Crimson started giggling in spite of herself. "You're not *that* old."

"Tell that to the scary person who hides in my mirror," Judy said lightly. "I'm ancient and I'm proud of it. I have love notes that Shakespeare wrote to me."

Judy's eyes stared into the depths of time, and she smiled. "I think the first thing your mom and I made together was cinnamon apple crumb pie. We were ten.

And the pie was a disaster! But boy, did we have fun baking it. Then of course Lenore became obsessed with pies and baked a new one practically every day."

"Ooh, I loved it when she invented some brand-new, totally wild pie creation that we'd never even heard of before!" said Crimson. "She always used to do that for my b—uh, special occasions."

"You can say the word 'birthday,' sweetie. You're going to be thirteen this year, fourteen the next, and so on and so on until you get like me—so old you run out of numbers big enough to count."

Judy got up to pour herself another cup of coffee, leaving the girls alone. The two friends just sat there silently, anxiously awaiting her return. Scarlett sipped her hot chocolate frantically, while Crimson fidgeted with her braids.

"You know," Judy said, sitting down, "your mom took birthdays very seriously. She believed that on those days you should think about your connection to other people. It may have been the day *your* journey started, but you joined lots who were already well along their own. Crimson, you're not drinking your hot chocolate," she added, more as an order than an observation.

Crimson sank even farther down in the booth, suppressing dozens of private thoughts she couldn't express. "I told you," she finally answered. "I didn't want anything."

"Well, I didn't ask you what you wanted. Any old short-order cook can serve what you *want*. I serve what you really *need*." She tilted her head and stared at them with one eye closed. "And my special Judy-senses tell me that what you need right now is a big cup of honesty, hold the denial. So drink up."

Judy eyed Crimson until she took her first sip,

and then turned back to Scarlett. "Now, where was I? Oh yes, see, Lenore believed that it wasn't enough just to accept birthday presents without a second thought. She always said that if you went out on your birthday—your own special day—and did something kind for a complete stranger without thought of reward, that would make you appreciate your presents all the more. She called it 'restocking the good fortune bank.'"

Crimson gave a soft whimper and closed her eyes. "Yeah, well, if you ask me, restocking the good fortune bank should have brought her a lot more good fortune than she ended up with."

"How can you say that?" Judy asked, dismayed. "That woman had more good fortune than most people dream of. Why, she had you, didn't she? And your father? And the bakery? She loved her life with you more than anything on this planet, and she felt blessed every day of her life to have you two."

"Yeah, I guess. But I always thought that the kind of person who restocked a fictitious good fortune bank would end up with more, you know? That's why I always believed in it—I thought it would pay off someday. But she didn't even have enough good fortune to keep her around long enough to . . . maybe she gave too much of it away. And now she's gone."

"Gone? *Gone*?" said Judy, her voice rising. "Look around you, Crimson. The smell of her muffins and cupcakes and pies is baked into these walls! Her baking made strangers smile. She brightened everyone's day, and not just with her delicious treats."

Scarlett leaned across the table to look her friend in the eye. "Look, Cee, I know this is really hard for you, but I think the last thing your mom would want is for you to go totally spla when there's work to do. Didn't she always tell us, 'Keep the hands busy while the mind solves the problems'? Besides, I know she would want you to celebrate your birthday. She'd want you to keep her traditions alive."

"Scarlett, I know you're just trying to help, but you don't understand. You couldn't possibly understand. I think we should just . . . let's just drop it. We have a lot to get done and it's already getting late."

At that, Judy looked up at the clock. "She's right about that. We have fourteen dinners to prepare for two shelters and a batch of Wheelie Meals for delivery. Hup, hup!"

TUESDAY
Lunchtime

Lunchtime on Tuesday at the Darq table turned into a buzz of students discussing their new volunteer projects. Emzie's hilarious tale of the dogpile on Scarlett at Frankie's Recycling Depot won Frankie half a dozen kids eager to sign up for the recycling fun. Crimson's crew arrived with a sketchbook full of designs for things they wanted to paint on their next set of fire hydrants. In no time at all, half the lunch period was gone.

It had been a while since the school participated in the kind of project that really got the students excited. Thanks to Community Service Week, instead of complaining about homework or the humdrum of their daily routine, Gen Fix was psyched to tackle the next volunteer assignment and eager to debate Harvest Fair booth ideas.

"So, Hawthorne, Ravencraft, how was the Cookin' Nook last night?" Pepper asked, pulling his shades down and eying the two girls. "Did you find out any juicy Old Mill gossip from the resident Beauty on Duty?"

"Oh, well—," Scarlett began.

"It was great!" Crimson jumped in, channeling some serious pep. "Judy is so amazing! She gave us free cups of her special hot chocolate, and then she told us all these seriously cool stories about the olden days, you know, when the café first opened and everything. Right, Ess?"

"Uh, yeah, Cee," Scarlett replied, slightly unsure of where all her friend's cheeriness had come from. "Seriously cool stories."

"Seriously cool?" Pepper questioned Scarlett. "Because it seems like you're seriously *confused*, my Darq friend."

"Confused?" Crimson chimed in. "Don't be insane. She's fine. Right, Ess? You're fine! Anyway, the Cookin' Nook was awesome, we can't wait to go back tonight."

Just then Winslow interrupted, "So, does *anybody* have any ideas about what we should do for the fair?"

"Ooh, what if we set up a video game console and charged a dollar a game?" Emzie shouted with excitement.

"What if DarqStarz gave a concert for charity— every hour on the hour?" Tara suggested.

"Yeah, that would be sweet!" Garrett chimed in.

A swell of discussion flowed down the table and back up again, debating the various booth suggestions. But by the time the end bell rang, all that had been decided was that everyone should post their ideas in the DarqSpace forum overnight and they would continue to debate the topic on Wednesday at lunch.

TUESDAY *Night*

Painting fire hydrants all afternoon had kept Crimson from fretting about the coming evening, but as she and Scarlett walked to Judy's afterward, her mind was churning a mile a minute. When they entered the Cookin' Nook, Judy called out her usual cheery greeting, but her attention was fixed on the large piles of food stacked up on the center table. There were plastic sandwich bags, paper lunch bags, sandwiches, bags of pretzels and potato chips, containers of pasta salad, apples, and juice boxes. Judy had already laid everything out, and it was time for the girls to get down to business.

Once all twenty meals were packed and set aside, Judy motioned for the girls to come sit at the counter stools, where two steaming cups of hot chocolate were waiting for them. Then she scooted behind the counter and pulled out a large photo album, which she spread open in front of them. "You have to see this."

As the girls slid onto their stools they saw that the album was filled with old pictures of young Judy and Lenore displaying their handiwork on the Cookin' Nook counter. "Lenore started out as a teenage waitress who wanted to learn to cook. Fancy food never really interested her, but once she discovered baking, she never looked back."

Judy turned the page to reveal a newspaper article featuring Lenore and a tray of frosted cupcakes, each one decorated with a cute little cat face painted in colored icing. "I remember those," Scarlett said. "She made humongous batches of them when we were little—each one was a different cat. She called them Cupcats. She made the most adorable one of Ruby Moon, do you remember, Cee?"

"Well, cupcakes *were* her most popular creations," Judy interjected. "She'd come into work and bake up five fresh batches of cupcakes, and not one lasted till lunch. The breakfast crowd bought them all. Then she'd be back in the kitchen baking up another five batches for the lunch crew. That's when I knew I had to help her open her own bakery." She looked at Crimson. "Cupcakes may have been her most *popular* treat, but they weren't her favorite. She always loved the thrill she got from inventing a new pie. But after she opened the bakery, she was so busy baking what was in high demand that she rarely had enough time to invent anything new. That's why she loved doing it on your bir—um, I mean, special occasions so much," Judy corrected herself, tossing a smile in Crimson's direction. "She'd look forward to that day for months at a time.

"Even when we were dead broke in the early days, Lenore could churn out a dozen different kinds of pies with whatever she found in the pantry. She could make sweet, fruity pies topped with whipped cream, breakfast pies with eggs, ham, or bacon, and lunch pies with creamy spinach and feta. You name it, and she could make a pie to put it in!"

Crimson looked reluctant, emotions churning behind her eyes. But she quickly glanced down at her watch, hoping that no one had noticed her choking up. "Maybe we should get going . . . it's already late and I still have some homework to do."

"You *need* this, darling," Judy said firmly. "I'm telling you, you gotta stop trying to hide how you're feeling and start expressing it! That's why your mom baked, you know. It's how she expressed herself. Now, I know you girls have all sorts of ways of doing that nowadays, with your websites and your rock music, but nothing beats cooking up a fresh batch of homemade goodies. And your mom knew that, all right. Every time something was bothering her, or you for that matter, she'd march right into her kitchen and bake up a brand-new pie—something she'd never tried before, something that didn't even come from a recipe. Well, I suppose it came from some kind of recipe in her head, but nothing that anyone had written down on paper."

"So, do you think that baking cures people, of, you know, like, problems?" Scarlett asked curiously.

"Well," said Judy, closing the album and brushing some crumbs off the tan leather cover. "It doesn't exactly cure anything, but it sure can make you feel better about whatever it is that's bugging ya! I mean, Lenore knew that the only way to cure a problem was to deal with it head-on, but the baking calmed her down and gave her some time to think about what was troubling her and how to deal with it. For her, the answer to those problems and how to deal with them was in the baking."

"In the baking, huh?" Scarlett repeated. "That's so cool. Isn't that so cool, Cee? Did you know that about your mom?"

"Of course I knew that!" Crimson erupted. "I mean, sorry, it's just . . . all this talk about my mom is making me feel weird. I think I should call it a night."

"Sure, sweetie," Judy said, putting the album away. "I know it's a lot to handle. But listen," she continued, reaching into a small tin box behind the counter. "I want you to have this. It's your mom's recipe for open-faced blasberry pie. It was her first ever pie creation—'blasberry' came from blending blackberries and raspberries together in this delicious, creamy filling. Anyway, I think she'd want you to have it. If you feel like baking it, bake it. If you don't, that's okay too. But I'm sure just holding on to it may do more for you than you think."

"Thanks, Judy," said Crimson, shoving the index card under her bag on the stool next to her.

"Well, thank you ladies for the help! It's a hoot having you back in here this week. I wish you'd come visit more often—and not just because of Service Week!" Judy told the girls. "But I know you're busy and whatnot."

"Thanks for telling us all those old stories, Judy," Scarlett said, pulling her scarf out of her bag. "It means a lot to . . . us."

"Yeah, thanks for everything. See you tomorrow!" Crimson called out, swinging her bag over her shoulder. In the shuffle, the recipe card flew off the stool, and Scarlett watched as it fluttered to the floor. She wondered if Crimson had noticed.

"Good night, girls." Judy waved, heading back into the kitchen.

As Crimson walked toward the exit, Scarlett quickly ducked down, swiped the worn-out recipe card that had wedged itself in between the floor and the counter's edge, and slipped it into her bag.

"Hurry up, Ess!" Crimson remarked, holding the

front door open. "It's cold out here."

"Sorry, Cee, just lacing up my boot."

A moment of silence passed as the two girls descended the front steps and began the walk from Judy's Cookin' Nook back home. "Hey, Cee, do you believe all that stuff, about finding the answer to life's problems in the baking?"

"I don't know, Ess. I mean, I guess my mom did, so I kinda have to believe it, right?"

"Yeah," Scarlett agreed resolutely. "That's what I thought too."

Later that night Crimson lay awake in bed, tossing and turning. She had way too much going on inside her head to sleep peacefully. It came as no surprise that she soon found herself sitting at her desk, the blue glow from her computer monitor the only light in her room, checking out the latest postings on DarqSpace. Mostly there were a bunch of comments on the two booth ideas that were tossed around at lunch: the video game and the DarqStarz concert.

She logged on to the DarqSpace private chat channel and was not surprised to see that Scarlett was also online.

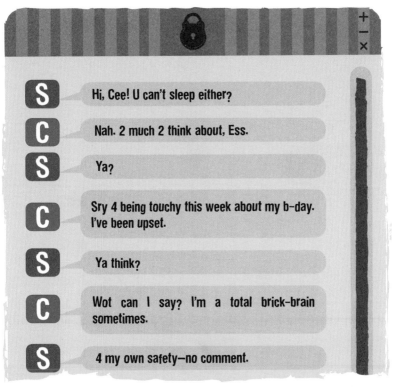

S — Hi, Cee! U can't sleep either?

C — Nah. 2 much 2 think about, Ess.

S — Ya?

C — Sry 4 being touchy this week about my b-day. I've been upset.

S — Ya think?

C — Wot can I say? I'm a total brick-brain sometimes.

S — 4 my own safety—no comment.

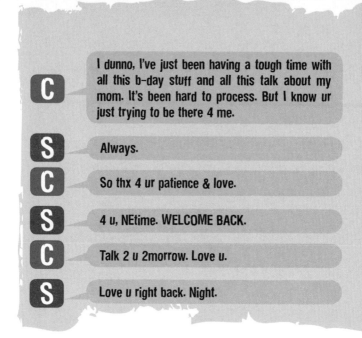

C I dunno, I've just been having a tough time with all this b-day stuff and all this talk about my mom. It's been hard to process. But I know ur just trying to be there 4 me.

S Always.

C So thx 4 ur patience & love.

S 4 u, NEtime. WELCOME BACK.

C Talk 2 u 2morrow. Love u.

S Love u right back. Night.

After signing off of DarqSpace, Scarlett felt a lot better about things between the two of them. Crimson had finally opened up—well, at least a little bit—and Scarlett believed now more than ever that her plan to help Crimson overcome everything was the perfect solution! It was just like Judy said: Sometimes people don't really know what they *need*. They may know what they *want*, but most of the time what they want and need aren't the same thing. Like, Judy knew that even though Crimson didn't *want* hot chocolate, she really *needed* it; and even though Crimson didn't really *want* to talk about her mom and her birthday, she really *needed* to start expressing her feelings. And that's why Judy gave Crimson the recipe card! It seemed pretty clear to Scarlett that Crimson was way too confused and upset to know what she *needed*, and it was her job as Crimson's best friend to figure it out for her. Scarlett had just promised her best friend that she would always be there for her, and that's exactly what she was going to do.

With her newfound confidence, Scarlett set her plan in motion. She went over to her bag and pulled out the recipe for Lenore's special open-faced blasberry pie. Then she signed back onto DarqSpace and posted her new idea for the Darq booth at the fair.

Fair Booth Idea #3 Lenore's Famous Pies

Hey Darqlings,
My idea for our booth is in honor of my favorite person in the whole world—Crimson—and her mom, Lenore. Lenore was a super-amazing baker and used to make these insanely creative and original pie inventions. I say, let's give Old Mill a taste of some good old-fashioned baker's secrets they'll never forget!

WEDNESDAY
Lunchtime

The Darqling table was abuzz when Crimson arrived at lunch the next day. Everyone seemed overly enthusiastic about something, and Crimson could only guess that someone had posted a really awesome idea for their booth late last night. While everyone was chitchatting, she decided to sign onto DarqSpace from her cell phone and find out what all the buzz was about.

Meanwhile, everyone at the table was frantically planning away, and Scarlett seemed to be at the center of the hubbub.

"Don't worry about costs, Scarlett," piped up Tara.

"We've got just about everything covered by freebies."

Garrett chimed in. "My aunt lives a few towns over, and her best friend works at this Italian bakery there. She said they'd give us all of their leftover flour, baking powder, sugar, and whatever other ingredients they've got lying around. Anything for a good cause, she said."

"And my grandma has this humongous garden. It's, like, acres of stuff," Emzie said. "If we get enough baskets, we can pick enough herbs, tomatoes, and other stuff to spice up anything—except maybe whatever the school serves us for lunch. Nothing can improve the taste of plastic."

"Boy, have I got you all beat," said Kaitlyn. "So, my sister's boyfriend's dad runs this dairy farm way out in the country. I talked to Jim—that's my sister's boyfriend—about getting his family to donate some of the dairy, like eggs, butter, and milk and stuff, and he said that his dad loves being the fuel that this town runs on, whatever that means, and that we can come by and take whatever doesn't get shipped off to stores!"

At that moment, Crimson, whose face was now redder than a bowl of fruit punch, stood up and stormed away from the table in a huff. Scarlett watched her friend fly out the double doors of the cafeteria and

was about to bolt after her when Winslow appeared, blocking her path. He brushed dog hairs off his flannel shirt and announced, a bit short of breath, "I stopped by Frankie's this morning—"

"Why did you do *that*?" Emzie interrupted.

Winslow screwed his face up in embarrassment. "I went to visit the dogs," he said almost inaudibly.

Emzie burst out laughing. "You—playing with non-CG animals! Wow! Cyber-Pinocchio is becoming a real boy!"

Winslow sniffed at her and backtracked to his original news. "Frankie says she's got at least three old ovens that people threw away, not realizing they only needed minimal tune-ups. She said we need a few extension cords and an outlet and then we're in business, which is no problem. We can request that the booth be by one of the buildings, and we can plug into their sockets." He raised his eyebrows at Emzie. "See, I *told* you there was stuff there that was too good to throw away."

Scarlett was excited to hear all the good news, but she was bursting at the seams to go see what was up with Crimson. "Winslow, that's great. Everyone, this is all totally incredible. It's looking like we're going to start making a profit the second the first slice is sold! But now, um, if you don't mind, I gotta go find Crimson. We can keep posting about this on DarqSpace later."

At that Scarlett grabbed her bag and rushed out of the cafeteria, heading straight for the girls' favorite spot—the old oak tree out by the sports fields—where she knew she'd find Crimson moping. Whatever it was had gotten Crimson in a real frenzy, and Scarlett couldn't bear the thought of her best friend being so upset.

"Hey, Cee," she called out to Crimson, who was sitting up against the tree with her head buried in her knees. "Is everything okay? What happened?"

"What happened?" Crimson asked in frustration, wiping the tears from her eyes. "You know exactly what happened, Scarlett—*you* did it!"

Scarlett's eyes opened wide in shock. "What do you mean, Cee? What did I do?"

"How dare you take that recipe and post it without asking me! That was my mom's recipe. Judy gave it to *me*—not you. It's just like how you didn't ask me if I wanted to celebrate my birthday. Do you even care what I want? Because it seems like you only care about what *you* want."

"I can't believe you're saying that," Scarlett replied, more hurt than she had ever felt before. "Of course I care, that's why I did it! You're upset and hurting and missing your mom, and it's . . . well, it's like Judy said. You think you want one thing, but you actually *need* something else, see? I'm trying to give you what you need. A chance to embrace your mom and something she loved. Judy said she found the answer in the baking, so I thought . . . I thought maybe you could too."

"No offense, Ess, but what makes you such an expert?" Crimson replied, even more fired up now than before. "You couldn't possibly begin to imagine what I'm feeling right now, or how hard this has been for me. What I needed was a friend to be there for me, to listen to what I wanted—and actually respect my wishes. Not someone who'd just ignore me completely and decide to do whatever she thought was best."

"I'm sorry, Cee. I'm sorry I hurt you, and I'm sorry you're so mad," Scarlett replied genuinely, tears starting to slowly fall from her eyes. "But I was really just trying to help. I thought this would make you happy. I thought it would help you remember your mom and enjoy your birthday again, knowing that we were keeping your

mom's traditions alive. But obviously I was wrong. I'll tell everyone to forget about the booth. I'll, um, I . . . I guess I'll just see you later. I really am sorry, Cee."

Scarlett wiped her eyes on her scarf one last time, turned on her heels, and walked back across the lawn toward the main building. Crimson watched as her best friend disappeared into the distance, wondering if things would ever be the same between them again.

When Scarlett got back to the Darq table, her friends were listening intently to Mac, who had apparently scored some gossip about the Leetz. "You'll love this, dudes," he said. "You know how blown away we were to hear that the Leetz volunteered for the sports field cleanup? Well, it turns out that their plan was to raid the elementary school and hire *fifth graders* to do the actual cleanup." That brought a burst of laughter from the table. "The kicker is—imagine what all those skateboard rats did when armed with leaf blowers and sharp-pointed litter sticks. The Leetz-dudes are already in debt for work the kiddies *didn't* do, and they still have to do the cleanup themselves. Oh, and the nurse's office wants them to buy a replacement carton for all the Band-Aids they used patching up the damage the kiddies did to each other."

The table erupted in laughter, but Scarlett could barely crack a smile. Emzie noticed her first. "Scarlett, did you hear that? Wait, is everything okay?"

"Actually, no. Sorry guys, but the pie booth idea is off. So please, just think of something else. Um, I gotta go."

And with that she was gone, leaving the rest of the Darqlings in a mass of confusion.

Later that evening, Scarlett was eager to get to the Cookin' Nook to see Crimson, hoping that they could use the time making meals to talk more calmly about the fight they'd had earlier. Maybe then things would finally go back to normal. But after forty-five minutes of waiting around, she realized that Crimson wasn't going to show up, and that she had perhaps done more damage to their friendship than she could have imagined.

"Judy, did you and Lenore ever get into a totally monstrous fight, one where, like, you stopped talking to each other?" Scarlett asked. Maybe she couldn't get any answers from Crimson, but that didn't mean she had to go home empty-handed.

"Oh sure, when we were young. We fought about lots of silly things, but in the end we always made up. That's what good friends do. Some fights are worse than others, but in the end we always knew that whatever happened, our intentions were true, and our hearts were in the right place."

"See, that's what I said!" Scarlett shouted out victoriously.

"Well, that may be true, but it doesn't mean that whatever you did didn't hurt Crimson, dear. It takes a big person to see beyond the hurt and recognize that, despite the end result, the intention was good. Crimson will get there, because she's that kind of person. But it may take her a little while."

"So you think I was wrong?" asked Scarlett, slightly confused.

"Well, honey, I'd have to know what you did in order to answer that question," Judy replied with a smirk.

"Ha, oh, right. Well, see, when you gave Crimson that recipe the other night, she kind of left it behind. So

I sort of took it and posted it on our website, suggesting that we make our booth for the fair a tribute to Lenore by baking all of her famous specialty pies. I thought it would be . . . I thought it would make Crimson happy."

"Oh, sweetie, that's probably one of the nicest and most thoughtful things anyone has ever done for Crimson. But boy, she must be pretty darn peeved at you, kid!"

"I don't understand. You just said it was sweet!"

"And it was. But Crimson, bless her heart, is way too emotionally charged to acknowledge that right now. Can't you see? She's sad, she's missing her mom, and she's trying to keep it all bottled up inside so no one can see it, and all the while you keep trying to drag it out of her. And then you go and send everyone this special recipe and set up this whole booth in memory of her mom and . . . well, you kind of stole Crimson's thunder right out from under her nose before she even realized it was there for the taking. And by the time she realized it was there, it was gone! Make sense?"

"Actually, that makes complete sense. Gosh, I'm such a dud! Will she ever forgive me?"

"You're not a dud, honey, you're the sweetest friend a girl could ask for. And the second Crimson figures that out, she's going to come a-runnin', I promise."

Later that night, Scarlett signed into the DarqSpace chat room, hoping to find Crimson online. Sadly, she was nowhere to be found, and after spending a half an hour online waiting for her, Scarlett finally called it a night. However, in another chat room on DarqSpace.com, a few other Darqlings were having a powwow of their own.

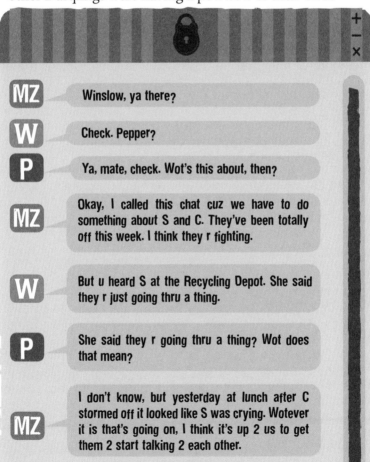

MZ Winslow, ya there?

W Check. Pepper?

P Ya, mate, check. Wot's this about, then?

MZ Okay, I called this chat cuz we have to do something about S and C. They've been totally off this week. I think they r fighting.

W But u heard S at the Recycling Depot. She said they r just going thru a thing.

P She said they r going thru a thing? Wot does that mean?

MZ I don't know, but yesterday at lunch after C stormed off it looked like S was crying. Wotever it is that's going on, I think it's up 2 us to get them 2 start talking 2 each other.

P So, wot do you suggest? An intervention?

MZ Kinda. At lunch tomorrow, I'll talk 2 S and try 2 convince her 2 talk 2 C. And Pepper, u do the same with C.

P I guess it's worth a shot. It does feel kinda girly, though, u sure you don't want 2 just talk 2 both of them?

MZ Nah, we need 2 tag team. Please?

P No prob. But what should we say?

MZ Def don't take sides. We just need 2 remind them that no matter what happened, they need 2 talk it out. That's what DarQ is all about, figuring things out no matter how confusing they seem, and stuff like that.

P Deal. If that doesn't make them feel guilty, I dunno wot will, LOL.

W Wot should I do?

MZ I think Pepper and I got it covered.

W So wot am I here for?

MZ Moral support. :)

So the three friends logged off, resolving to do whatever they could to bring their favorite two Darqlings back together.

If an intervention was what Scarlett and Crimson needed, that was exactly what they would get.

Still unwilling to talk to Scarlett, despite Pepper's pleading session

THURSDAY
Evening

Still unwilling to talk to Scarlett, despite Pepper's pleading session at lunchtime, Crimson decided to rearrange her shifts after school that day. Though she had to admit that there was something to Pepper's whole "Darq is about talking things out" speech, she wasn't quite there yet. So she spent the afternoon bagging dinners at the Cookin' Nook with Judy, and the evening painting fire hydrants with Pepper and Mac—who both knew better than to bring up anything birthday-, pie-, or Scarlett-related again.

It was strange to think that she'd actually gone a

whole day without talking to or seeing her best friend. They had never done that before, and she felt like there was a whole part of her missing. But she desperately tried to put it out of her mind.

On her way home from the park, where she had finished her last hydrant of the evening, she decided to make a very special stop. Taking the dirt path that began in her backyard, she followed it until she reached

an old wrought-iron gate. There she wove her way past worn marble monuments until she reached the plot that held her mom's grave. Its inscription had faded a bit in the last year and a half, but the stone letters still had their crisp edges.

LENORE
HAWTHORNE

Beloved
Wife
And
Mother

"To Live in the Hearts
of Those You Love
Is Not to Die"

"Hey, Mom," Crimson began, sitting down in front of the grave and crossing her legs. "So, it's been kind of a crazy week, huh? I'm sure you've been watching, I mean, I guess you have. Actually, I don't really know how that whole thing works. Anyway, I've been learning a lot about you from Judy, so that's been really nice. I never realized how totally talented you were, but Judy says people would, like, line up outside the bakery just for a cupcake. And to think I used to get all the cupcakes I wanted. . . . Anyway, I guess I've just been missing you a lot, and I've been thinking that this year you won't be inventing a special 'Crimson Turns Thirteen' birthday pie, which I've, like, dreamt about since I was little. I guess I thought that maybe if I didn't turn thirteen, you know, maybe if I just didn't celebrate my birthday at all, that would make me miss you and your special pie a little less. But maybe Scarlett was right about something, because if I know you, you're probably furious that I'm even *thinking* about skipping my birthday, huh? She said you'd want me to celebrate and keep your traditions alive . . . you probably agree with her on that one."

"Well," called a voice from behind her. "I know I

agree with her. Does that count for something?" said Nat Hawthorne, making his way through the crunchy leaves and crouching down next to his daughter. He was carrying a cheerful arrangement of bright flowers in a plain vase. "Is it okay if I share the sunset with you and Mom?"

"Of course," Crimson answered. "So you heard what I was saying, then, huh?"

"The tail end of it, yeah. And I know Mom, and she would be so upset if she knew you were thinking of trying to forget your birthday this year. This is a big birthday, sweetie, and there's no way I'm letting you go without celebrating. And Scarlett's a good friend—always has been—and she knows better than to let you get away with that."

"Yeah, well, things with Scarlett aren't so wonderful these days."

"Well, I'm sure whatever it is, you two girls will work things out. I never saw two friends as close as you are, except maybe Lenore and Judy. I trust that you'll figure it out, Crimson. You're a smart cookie, you are.

"You know, before your mom," he continued, looking up at the sun setting, "I used to think that sunsets were sorta sad. Every day, the poor old sun seemed to sink into the horizon as the dark won out over the light. But then your mom pointed out that the day *had* to give way to night so that the sun could race around the rest of the planet as fast as it could, so it would be there, bright and yellow, to bring us a brand-new day."

"Wow, Dad. That sounds just like the Darq philosophy we came up with."

Nat's face broke into a tired smile. "What?" he said. "You thought you and Scarlett *invented* all that?" He chuckled gently.

Silence descended on them as they watched the light fade, and the earliest stars grew brighter than the indigo sky.

"Dad?"

"Yes?"

"Even if I can move past it all, and be okay living life . . . without her, it doesn't seem right that I should be *happy*, celebrating something silly like a birthday party . . . when she can't be . . . happy with me."

"What makes you think she's *not* happy, sweetheart?"

"Well . . . well, I dunno, I guess. I mean, she's gone, and I can't feel if she's happy or not anymore."

"You not being able to feel her happiness probably says more about your limits than hers. I can honestly assure you that Mom is *very* happy."

After a moment, he added, "Her greatest joy was seeing other people happy. That's why she loved having her own bakery. It gave her a big charge to see a customer bite into a goodie and break out into a giant, crumb-spilling smile."

"Yeah, that's kinda what Judy said. So you think she would want me to celebrate, then, and keep her traditions alive?"

"I think you know the answer to that one already, sweetie."

"So Scarlett was right, then?" Crimson prodded again.

Nat chuckled, putting his arm around his daughter's shoulders and squeezing her tightly. "I think you know the answer to that one too."

And as the sunset faded into a creamy red glow on the horizon and twilight fully claimed the sky, Nat and Crimson clasped hands and walked back up to the house.

That morning Crimson awoke bright and early, planning to ride her bike to Scarlett's house before school. She had been bursting with excitement all night long, eager to make up with her best friend and put all of this glum behind her. She even had a peace offering in hand. On her way to Scarlett's she had stopped off at the Cookin' Nook and gotten two cups of Judy's special hot chocolate—to go. Crimson made her way up the long and winding driveway and rang Scarlett's doorbell.

Scarlett answered the door. "Cee! What are you doing here?"

"I come in peace," she said, offering up a mini curtsy and presenting the cup of steaming hot chocolate as proof.

"Mmmm . . . this stuff is addictive," Scarlett said, lifting the lid off her cup and taking a sip.

"Judy keeps saying there's no secret ingredient, but I don't believe her for a second. I mean, chocolate is good . . . but not *this* good." Crimson commented. "So . . ."

"Yeah, so . . ."

"Look, Ess, I'm really sorry I went so ballistic on you. You were only trying to help, and you had all these great ideas, but I was so dead set on being a total Grinch that I just shot them all down."

"No way. It was my fault, Cee!" Scarlett yelped, barely able to keep the hot chocolate from spilling out of her mouth. "I, like, knew you had all this thunder you wanted, and instead of giving it to you, I totally stole it away, and now you're thunderless!"

"I, uh, hmmm . . . what are you talking about? How am I thunderless?"

"You know, because I stole your thunder! Judy said that you didn't really want to be a grump but that

you didn't know how to deal with it all, and instead of helping you, I, like, swooped in and stole all these great ideas, aka your thunder, and orchestrated the whole pie booth thing without even involving you in it, thereby leaving you thunderless."

"Judy said I was thunderless?"

"I'm paraphrasing. Whatever, look, it doesn't matter what she said, what matters is that she was totally right, and I didn't realize how wrong I was at the time, but I do now. I'm so sorry, Cee. It was really wrong of me to stomp all over your toes like that."

"Wow, that's ironic, because I came all the way over here to tell you that actually, *you* were right. I had no idea what I needed, and I was so focused on being sad and angry that I couldn't see what was right in front of me—the best way ever to celebrate my mom *and* my birthday—but you did. And you were just hoping that it would make me happy. And if I wasn't such a dud I would have seen that."

"So that makes us both pretty lame, huh?" Scarlett added, laughing.

"Yeah, I guess so. Maybe we should have paid a little more attention to our Darq philosophy this week."

"Funny, that's exactly what Emzie said to me at lunch yesterday!"

"And what Pepper said to me!"

"Hmm . . . it seems our little Darqling friends have played us, Cee. Using our own words, no less."

"Well it's about time. I was beginning to wonder if they were learning anything!" Crimson joked. "So," she continued, "this isn't a total loss, at least not yet. We still have till tomorrow to pull off the best pie-baking booth ever. You in?"

Scarlett smiled widely. "I'm in—on one very crucial condition: You can't give us any lip about what we may or may not do for your birthday. Deal?"

"Wow, well done. You always do get your way, don't you?"

"I *am* a Ravencraft," Scarlett replied slyly.

"Okay, you've got a deal. Now, don't we have some pies to bake or something?"

As the girls rode their bikes to school, Scarlett filled Crimson in on all the help that their friends had rounded up: the herbs and vegetables, the dairy, the flour and sugar and baking powder, the refurbished ovens—all of which were being donated by various friends of friends.

Now all they needed was to get some more of Lenore's recipes from Judy, buy whatever ingredients hadn't been donated, and start baking. The girls had a very long day ahead of them, but they couldn't wait for it to begin!

SATURDAY Afternoon

The Darq crew had spent the whole of Friday evening gathering supplies and ingredients, and most of Saturday morning preparing the first four pies in their respective homes. Garrett and Kaitlyn tackled Lenore's special cinnamon apple crumb pie; Pepper, Tara, and Mac prepared her famous bacon, brie, and egg breakfast pie; Winslow and Emzie conquered the chocolate mousse surprise pie; and Scarlett and Crimson, of course, handled Lenore's first creation ever: open-faced blasberry pie.

Scarlett and Crimson arrived at the town square

around noon, just as the city workers were blocking off the side streets with sawhorses. Crimson waved at the crew. "You guys work too hard," she called out to them as she and Scarlett passed by in Nat's car. "Stop by Lenore's Famous Pies for some freebies to rebuild your strength!"

Scarlett blinked. "You're giving away free pieces of pie before we've even sold any?"

"Sure, why not?" replied Crimson. "Sharing without expectation of reward, that was my mom's thing, according to Judy." She flashed an impish grin. "Besides, someone's got to eat the test batches."

They reached their booth site just as the rest of their crew was unloading the last equipment from Frankie's battered pickup truck.

"Our fearless leaders finally arrive!" Pepper announced when he saw them. "Your timing is perfect—all the heavy lifting just finished. Oh, and Hawthorne, happy birthday!"

"Yeah, Cee," Scarlett chimed in. "Happy birthday—*again!*" Satisfied that she could now tease her best friend about her birthday to no end without consequence, Scarlett enjoyed any and every opportunity to do so, and invited all their other friends to join in. "Before all this craziness begins, I want to give you your birthday present," she continued, handing Crimson a neatly wrapped, square-shaped box.

"Aw, Ess, you didn't have to get me anything! Forgiving me was already way nice of you."

"Yeah, well, I'm just raising the bar for when my birthday comes along," Scarlett replied jokingly.

Crimson reached for the box and carefully unwrapped the package. Inside was her very own leather-bound album, and in it Scarlett had handwritten all of Lenore's pie recipes that they had gotten from Judy, along with some old pictures of Lenore at the Cookin' Nook, in her own bakery, and at home with Crimson on various birthdays.

"I thought it might be nice for you to have your own book of memories," Scarlett added.

"Ess, this is the best present I've ever gotten," Crimson told her, giving her best friend a big hug. "What would I do without you?"

"Do you really want me to answer that?" replied Scarlett sarcastically.

"Actually, on second thought, nah."

After the birthday cheers, the gang got down to business setting up their booth. As Crimson looked at the bustling setup for the Harvest Fair block party, it seemed she was seeing everything through a very different set of eyes than she'd started out with at the beginning of the week. Modern life had turned into this constant blizzard of information, images, stimulations, and sensations from the outside that slammed into the swirling storm of thoughts, ideas, emotions, and urges that were already banging around in her skull. The penalty for not getting some kind of grip on life was the very real and very scary threat of Losing It Big-Time. And she realized that this week she kinda *had* lost it big-time—but thankfully her friends were right there to help her get back on track.

When she and Scarlett had first talked about the Darq, about creating a world and philosophy to help deal with life, it was precisely for weeks like the one she'd just had—where everything was so super crazy that it was easy to lose track of your sense of self and balance. And sure enough, when she lost track of herself and everything else, it was Darq that brought it back. It wasn't just something that she and Scarlett talked about in the Lair anymore. Even if they hadn't exactly invented it, even if her mom and Judy, and even her dad, had kinda been living it for a while already, she and Scarlett were still doing their part to keep it alive and pass it on. And it was enough to spark a website, and a band. And that spark blazed into a totally cool song, and like moths, complete strangers were drawn to that new light, close enough to find themselves part of a crowd of similar strangers. Then a huge smile spread across Crimson's face as she realized that no matter what craziness life threw at her, she'd always be able to find her way back.

Crimson walked across the square from where the booth was being set up and watched the progress. Tara and Kaitlyn had created tables by laying planks on sawhorses and then stapling plastic tablecloths over them. They had painted LENORE'S FAMOUS PIES on the tablecloth and set out hand-lettered cards listing the varieties of pies they would be selling at the tables. Winslow and Frankie were setting up the ovens and organizing the extension cords to reach into the nearest building. Once that was settled, everyone popped the first pie they had brought into the ovens and got down to work preparing the second round of flavors. There was lemon-sugar tart pie, caramel apple and pear pie, crabcake pie, and countless others that the gang couldn't wait to try.

Crimson looked over at her dad, who was hanging out with the crew behind the booth, helping with the ovens. She wondered how he was feeling about all of this—if it was making him miss Mom even more. She hoped that even if it was, it was also helping him remember her better too. She thought about how much her mom used to love Community Service Week—and the fair that marked the end of it. It was her favorite school-enforced extracurricular activity because it endorsed the idea of giving back to the community that she always tried to impress on her family.

Crimson looked around at all the hardworking people and realized what it was about giving back that her mom loved so very much. This project had brought together total strangers to work toward brightening the lives of other total strangers.

enore's
Famous Pies

A questioning look from Scarlett brought Crimson's brain back to the here and now. "Hey, Cee, you okay?"

"Better than okay. Hey, you know how my mom always talked about giving back to the good fortune bank, and how amazing that feeling was?" Crimson asked with a warm smile. "Well, I think I finally just experienced that feeling."

For the first time, Crimson understood that maybe tangible things like pies weren't the only things that could remind her of her mom. There were tons of things all around her that had the power to do that, including maybe even Crimson herself.

SATURDAY Evening

It was late in the afternoon before Scarlett and Crimson finally got a chance to poke their heads up for air. They looked at each other and realized that the day had become a total blur, the only constant being the frenzy the crowd seemed to be experiencing over Lenore's pies. Crimson would have been willing to swear that the entire population of Old Mill and the New Mill suburbs had shown up to buy a slice of pie. Twice. Now it looked like the town was lining up for a third go, or someone was trucking in people from other towns. It was time for a break. Rinsing their hands off, the two girls staggered out to see what else was at the fair besides pie.

The goal of the Harvest Fair was to raise money for a good cause—and this year's proceeds were going to help upgrade the local library's computer lab. The town and schools were raising money through booth fees and a cut of their sales. Throughout the afternoon the mayor had been walking around from booth to booth, taking polls on how much money people had raised for the cause. By midafternoon, the community had already reached its ten-thousand-dollar goal, and ten Community Service Stars had been awarded—one of which had gone to the Lenore's Famous Pies booth for creativity and greatest ratio of money earned to money spent.

Not for the first time that day, Crimson wondered where Judy was. This was her natural element, and she hadn't shown up yet. "Hey, Ess, do you know where Judy is? I thought she would have shown up hours ago."

"Hmm . . . sorry, Cee, I don't. You didn't see her at the Cookin' Nook booth?"

"Nope, and everyone there seemed pretty tight-lipped about where she was."

"That's odd. Well, I'm sure she'll turn up soon. Maybe there was a cooking emergency or something."

As the girls walked, Crimson pointed across the square. "May I direct you to the Leetz's latest attempt to win a place in the Guinness Book of Epic Fail."

"Oh, my . . . ," Scarlett said. As she might have expected, the Leetz booth was a total exercise in Over. As in Overstated, Overdone, and Over the Top.

The booth was clearly borrowed from some Leet's corporate dad. It might have passed without notice at a sales convention, but its flimsy prefab construction and space-age plastic made it stand out like a visitor from Planet Polyester.

Crimson nudged Scarlett's rib. "It looks like the Decorating Committee couldn't agree on anything—"

5$ kisses 5$

"So they each did something different," agreed Scarlett. "With sunglasses on."

"How are the jocks going to get all that *glitter* off, Ess? And excuse me, but how much money did they have to spend to make it look like that anyway?"

"Oh, you're excused," Scarlett teased.

"I think all that glitter is blinding me," Crimson joked back. "My poor eyes."

"What has been seen cannot be unseen, my child," Scarlett said, pulling Crimson back the other direction.

They were still giggling and acting stunned when they reached the pie booth. Pepper looked up. "You just came from the Leetz's kissing booth, I presume."

"Barely survived to tell the tale," Scarlett said, holding out shaking hands.

"We didn't see anyone but the Leetz at the booth," said Crimson. "Kisses for cash not all it's cracked up to be?"

Pepper snorted. He looked at them again, more seriously this time. "Take a wild guess at what their moneymaking scheme was."

"Let's see," Crimson began. "They're greedy, lazy, they have galaxy-size egos . . . honestly, nothing could shock me."

Everyone in the crew gathered in close to tell the tale at the same time:

"They really thought—"

"— that guys would pay—"

"—five bucks—"

"—for a kiss—"

"—on a piece of paper—"

"—made by a red ink RUBBER STAMP!"

The whole crew doubled over with laughter.

Before Scarlett and Crimson had a chance to comment, they heard a roar from the street as a large truck pulled up right next to the pie booth. Crimson recognized the truck—it had the name of her mother's bakery on it: Heaven-Sent Baked Goods.

Inside the truck were baking racks upon baking racks of something that carried the smell of wonderfulness to everyone at the booth. Scarlett and Pepper leaped forward to drop the loading ramp from the back of the truck. Vaguely familiar-looking people climbed out of the truck and started rolling the racks down to ground level. Finally Judy stepped out of the driver's seat, followed by Crimson's favorite (and only) Aunt Roxi, who had come to join in the festivities. Judy had made it after all—and she had brought some baked goods with her.

"Attention, everybody," Judy boomed. "We all know how important this day is for all those people who are being helped by your generosity. But there's another reason that this is an important day."

She extended a hand toward Crimson. "Today is the birthday of my best friend's daughter, Crimson Hawthorne. Now, Crimson, we know you started off the week wanting

absolutely no mention of your birthday . . . but then we found out from a little birdie—whose name starts with an S—that you are under orders not to give anyone any lip about how we choose to celebrate this great day. So, I hereby wish you a very happy thirteenth birthday, Crimson, and offer up a token of your mom's love to sweeten the deal.

"The fine bakers who run Lenore's bakery are part of her legacy. Not only do they continue to run it, but they still make most of her signature creations. And they have baked some of those delicious treats for this very special occasion." Judy signaled the bakers to start

bringing trays from the racks. "Ladies and gentlemen, in honor of Crimson's birthday, I present you with Lenore Hawthorne's famous cupcakes—the best birthday present anyone could wish for! We even brought back some of Lenore's super special Cupcats, for nostalgia's sake."

Crimson was frozen in shock, her mouth stuck in a dumbstruck grin even as Scarlett gave her a bone-crushing hug and a kiss on her cheek.

"How did you manage to pull this off on such short notice?" asked Crimson.

"I'm a *Ravencraft*. How many times do I have to tell you this?" Scarlett replied, pretending to sulk.

"All right, all right, you're a *Ravencraft*. Now if I could only get my last name to have some kind of superpower, we could be a wicked duo, don't ya think?"

"I think we kinda already are, Cee."

And with that, Crimson grabbed Scarlett's hand and they went dashing into the fray, muscling forward toward the birthday treats. "Birthday girl gets first dibs!" Crimson shouted. "Step aside, ladies and gents, there's a Ruby Moon Cupcat with my name on it!"